P9-BYX-448

First published by Parragon in 2010

Parragon
Queen Street House
4 Queen Street
Bath BA1 1HE, UK

ISBN 978-1-4454-1502-4

Printed in China

The Wizard of Oz

Based on the story by L. Frank Baum
Illustrated by Amanda Gulliver

Parragon

Bath • New York • Singapore • Hong Kong • Cologne • Delhi
Melbourne • Amsterdam • Johannesburg • Auckland • Shenzhen

Dorothy and her little dog, Toto, lived in Uncle Henry and Aunt Em's house in Kansas. One day, a strong wind swept up the house. It was set down in a magical land. Lots of strange little people lived there.

"I am the Good Witch of the North," a beautiful woman said to Dorothy. "I would like to thank you for killing the Wicked Witch of the East, and for setting us free."

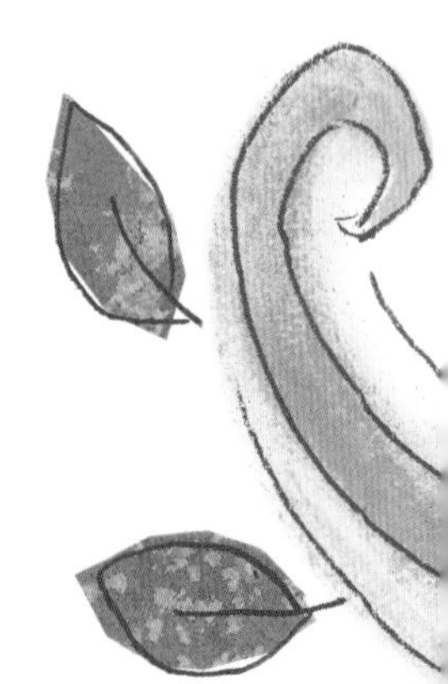

"I have not killed anyone," gasped Dorothy.

"Well, your house did," replied the good witch. And she pointed to two red shoes sticking out from the corner of the house.

"Oh, dear! Oh, dear!" cried Dorothy.

"Don't worry, she was a very wicked witch," explained the good witch. "Now her magic shoes are yours. She was very proud of them but no one knows how they work. Here, put them on."

Dorothy wanted to go back home. The good witch had never heard of Kansas.

"You will have to go to the Emerald City and ask Oz," said the good witch.

"He is a great wizard. He will know how you can get back to Kansas."

"How do I get to the Emerald City?" asked Dorothy.

"Just follow the yellow brick road," said the good witch.

Dorothy and Toto found the yellow brick road. After they'd been walking for a long time they stopped beside a scarecrow for a rest.

The scarecrow winked. "Would you help me down from this pole?" he said.

Dorothy had never heard a scarecrow speak before! She helped the scarecrow down.

Dorothy said she was on her way to see the Wizard of Oz.

"Perhaps he could give me some **brains** to replace the straw in my head," said the scarecrow.

All three set off together along the yellow brick road.

Further along the road they saw a man made of tin.
He couldn't move because his joints were rusted.

"Help!" groaned the tinman. "Oil my joints with that oil can."

Dorothy oiled his joints so he could move.

"We're going to the Emerald City to see the Wizard," explained Dorothy. "He's going to send me back to Kansas."
"And he's going to give me a brain," added the scarecrow.

"Could he give me a **heart**?" asked the tinman.
"I expect so," said Dorothy.
"Then I'll come too," he decided.

Suddenly, a huge lion jumped out and knocked the scarecrow to the ground. Toto barked and the lion went to bite him.

ROOAAARRRR

"You coward!" Dorothy cried. "A great beast like you trying to bite a tiny dog."

"I'm just a big **scaredy cat,"** sobbed the lion. "I haven't got any courage."

The lion decided to join them on their quest to seek Oz's help.

The new friends continued on until they arrived at the Emerald City.

Dorothy rang a bell and the gate swung open.
"I am the gatekeeper. What do you want?" said a soldier.
"We've come to see the Wizard," explained Dorothy.
"Oz is a great but terrible wizard. If you are dishonest or nosy, he could destroy you. You must take care."
They followed the gatekeeper to the Palace of the Great Oz.

The gatekeeper went to tell the great Oz that he had visitors. When he returned he said Oz would see them one at a time. Dorothy went in first. In the middle of the room a head floated above an emerald throne.

"I am Oz, the great and terrible,"

roared the head. "What do you want?"

"I am Dorothy the small and meek. I want you to send me back to Kansas."

"Only if you kill the Wicked Witch of the West, like you did the Wicked Witch of the East," said the head.

"But that was an accident, how can I kill a witch?" wailed Dorothy.

"I don't know," replied the head. "But don't come back until you do."

Feeling very sad, Dorothy went back to tell her friends what the wizard wanted her to do.

When the scarecrow went to see Oz, he saw a beautiful lady sitting on the throne. He asked her for brains and she replied that he must help Dorothy kill the Wicked Witch of the West.

When the tinman visited the room, he saw a terrible beast, with five eyes, and a huge body. When he asked for a heart, he was told the same.

Lastly, the lion went in. He saw a huge ball of fire. It told him that if he wanted courage he must destroy the Wicked Witch.

"We will have to do as he asks," said Dorothy to her friends.

"Good luck," said the gatekeeper, pointing out the path to the witch's castle.

The friends didn't realize that they were being watched by the Wicked Witch. She only had one eye but it was very powerful. When she saw the uninvited guests, she was furious. She shouted, "Ziz-zy, zuz-zy, zik!"

Winged monkeys immediately surrounded her.

“Destroy the tinman and the scarecrow,” she commanded. “And bring me the others.”

The winged monkeys found Dorothy and her friends. Some seized the tinman and the scarecrow and dropped them into a deep ravine. Others caught Dorothy, Toto, and the lion, and carried them to the witch’s castle.

The witch was frightened when she saw Dorothy wearing the red shoes. The witch said some magic words and Dorothy fell over.

One shoe flew off and the witch snatched it. Dorothy threw a bucket of water over the witch. The witch shrieked and melted away. The winged monkeys took Dorothy and her rescued friends back to the Emerald City.

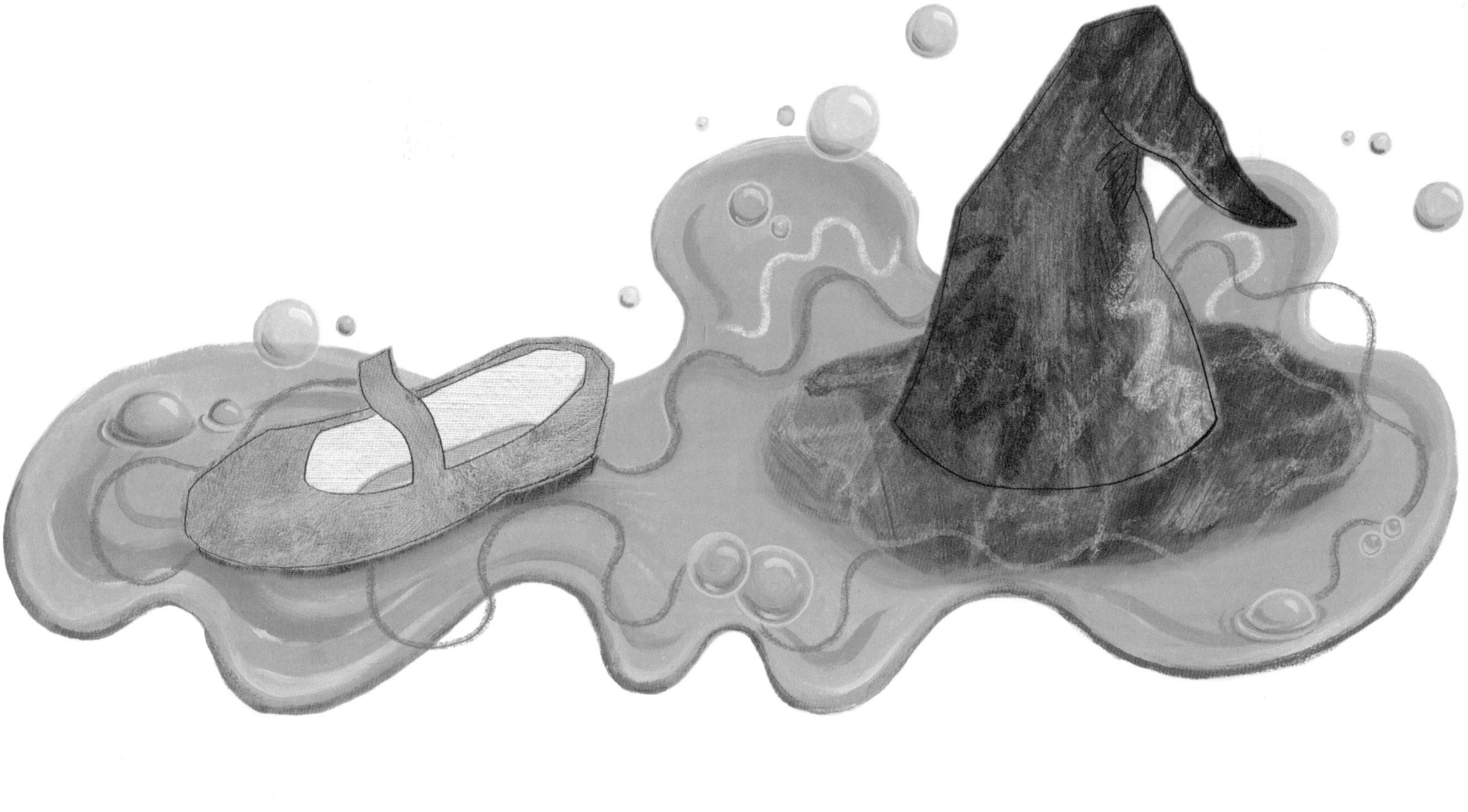

The friends rushed into Oz's throne room.

"What do you want?" said a voice.

"We have destroyed the Wicked Witch of the West," said Dorothy. "We want what you promised us."

"Err . . . come back tomorrow," said the voice.

The lion roared. Toto jumped in alarm and knocked over a screen to reveal a little man.

"Who are you?" cried the tinman.

"I am Oz, the great and terrible," squeaked the little man. "Or rather I've been pretending to be. I accidentally flew here in a hot air balloon."

"So you can't give us what you promised," cried Dorothy.

"I can still help you," he said. And he gave the scarecrow a special stuffing for brains. He gave the tinman a red silk heart. And he gave the lion a drink to give him courage.

"How will I get to Kansas?" asked Dorothy.

"We'll fly there in my hot air balloon," said the little man.

Dorothy, Toto, and the wizard climbed into a hot air balloon. As the balloon rose into the air, Toto leapt out of the basket, so Dorothy jumped out after him. The balloon flew away, leaving Dorothy and Toto behind.

"I'll never see Uncle Henry and Aunt Em again," sobbed Dorothy. Then suddenly, a woman appeared, "I am the Good Witch of the South," she smiled. "How can I help you?"

"Help me get back to Kansas," pleaded Dorothy.

"Your red shoes will carry you," said the witch. "Just knock the heels together three times."

Dorothy thanked the witch. Then she picked up Toto and tapped her shoes together three times.

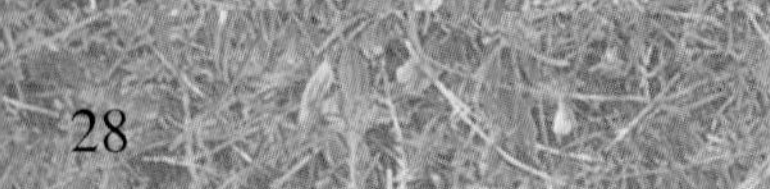

"Take me home to Aunt Em!" she said.

She was whirled through the air and the next thing she knew she was back home in Kansas. Dorothy's adventure was over at last. Aunt Em dropped her watering can and rushed over.

"Aunt Em!" cried Dorothy.

"I'm so glad to be home."